Dr. Roger Moore

Richelle Clementeon

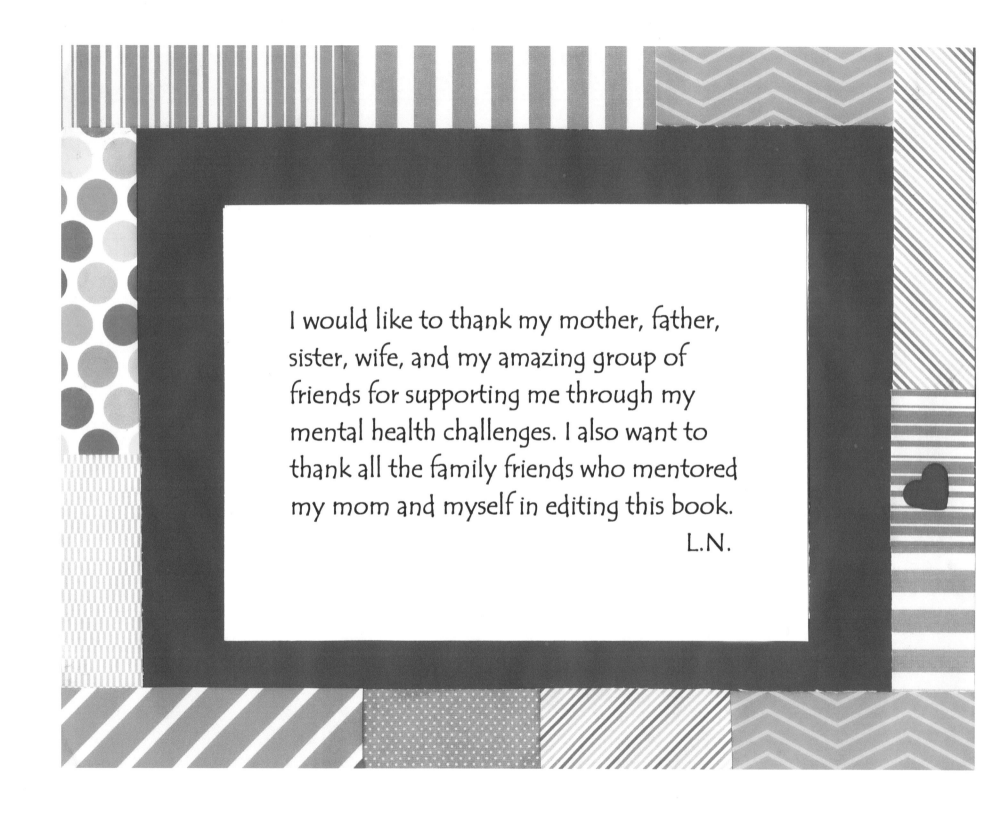

I would like to thank my mother, father, sister, wife, and my amazing group of friends for supporting me through my mental health challenges. I also want to thank all the family friends who mentored my mom and myself in editing this book.

L.N.

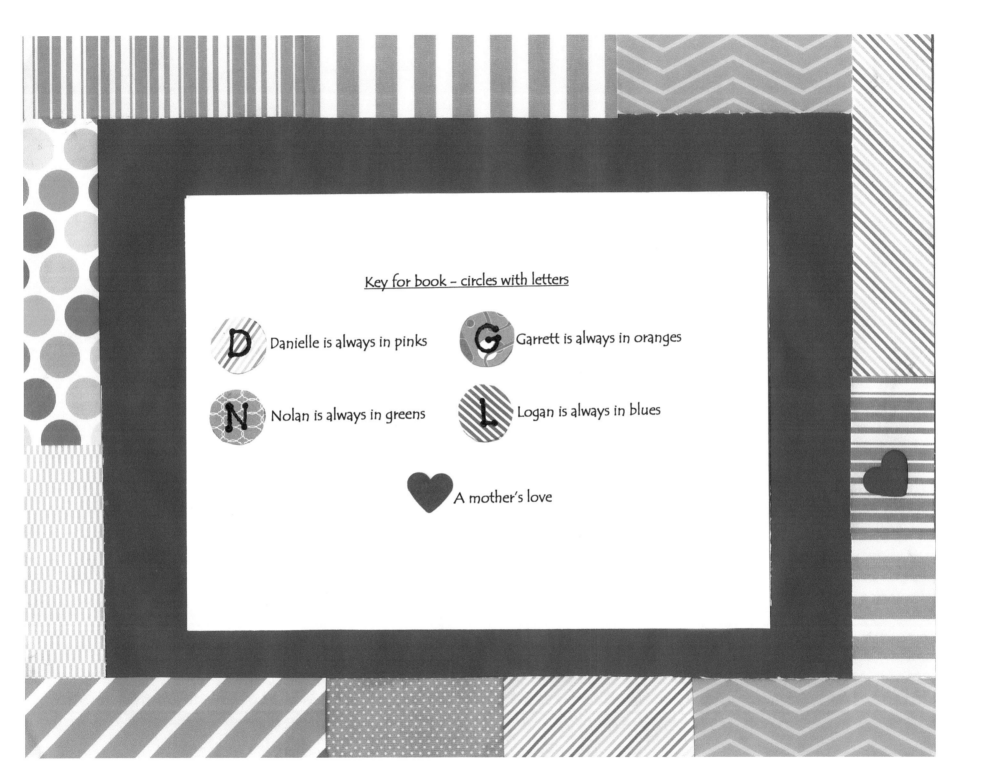

Key for book – circles with letters

D Danielle is always in pinks

G Garrett is always in oranges

N Nolan is always in greens

L Logan is always in blues

♥ A mother's love

We ALL have Something

Story by Logan Noone

Pictures by his mom, Rochelle Clementson

Logan moved to a new town when he was in Third Grade. Logan worried he would not have any friends. His parents told him he would make friends quickly by being friendly and playing games at recess.

Logan quickly became best friends with Garrett, Danielle, and Nolan. The four friends played basketball, skied, and skateboarded all the time. Logan felt happy and always laughed and smiled with his new best friends.

That first winter, Logan broke his leg playing basketball and couldn't play sports. He had his friends sign his cast and couldn't wait until he could start playing with them again. As the weeks went on, though, he felt sad sitting alone inside watching them playing together outside during recess.

After two months, the doctor removed Logan's cast and he started walking around. Logan was happy and would laugh with his three best friends all the time.

The next year, Logan was excited to be a Fourth Grader along with Danielle, Garrett, and Nolan. He didn't know why, but that winter he began to feel sad again. Logan was confused. Why wasn't he happy? He didn't have a broken leg, and he had lots of friends at school. He just felt blue and was too embarrassed to tell anyone. During this time, Logan's parents, friends, and teachers all sensed something wasn't right about Logan.

Logan had always loved skiing with his friend Danielle. One snowy day in December, Logan sat by the window feeling sad and lonely. Suddenly he heard a knock at the door. "Hey Logan" Danielle yelled after she took off her coat. "It's snowing, let's go skiing!" "I don't know, Danielle." Logan sounded tired and had none of his usual energy. "I just don't seem to want to do anything these days but my mom just took me to a doctor to talk about how I have been feeling."

Danielle laughed out loud, "I see doctors all the time! It's not fun, but I don't let it stop me from skiing." "What do you mean? You look healthy," said Logan. Danielle answered quickly, "I had cancer a few years ago. I am happy and proud that I have been cancer free for two years." Logan was shocked. He felt better knowing someone else who had to go to the doctor too.

"What about you? Is everything okay?" asked Danielle. "Well, I haven't really felt myself lately. I've felt sad, lonely, and out of energy. The doctor said that these feelings are called depression and it just happens sometimes. To feel better, I should do things I like, especially exercise!" "What!" Danielle said. "You used to love to ski and that's a form of exercise. We went all the time last year. Remember how much fun we had?" Logan wasn't convinced so Danielle tried again. "Logan, the snow is perfect right now. Try skiing for five minutes and if you aren't having fun, we'll come back inside."

Logan decided to give it a try. He climbed up to the top of the hill and took his first run, finishing with a massive smile on his face. Logan and Danielle built a jump near the bottom of the hill, and skied the whole afternoon. "Wow, time really flies when you are having fun doing something you love!" he thought. Logan and Danielle continued to ski throughout the winter, even when he felt a little sad, because *now* he knew that exercise helped him feel happier.

The four friends were now Fifth Graders. Logan and Garrett were going to try out for the basketball team. Logan couldn't wait to play but he started worrying, "What if I break my leg again?" Logan became quiet again and couldn't sleep at night. His mind would not rest.

One day Garrett came by and said, "Let's go shoot some hoops. Basketball tryouts are soon." "I don't know if I am going to play this year," replied Logan. "I worry about breaking my leg again and I can't sleep at night." "But you love basketball, Logan," said Garrett. "I know," answered Logan sadly. "So, my mom took me to the doctor and he told me that I have anxiety. He thinks I should try some breathing exercises and meditation. Maybe it will help."

"My doctor told me to use breathing exercises along with meditation to help with my heart condition!" said Garrett. Logan was confused. He had no idea Garrett had a heart condition. "I was born with heart problems. I've had three surgeries so far. My doctor taught me that meditation can help slow down my heart rate. I use it after I exercise and when I get worried."

"Let's try it right now," Garrett suggested. "Meditate? How do we do that?" Logan replied. "It's easy! I have a recording on my phone. All we have to do is sit, close our eyes, and listen. We focus on our breathing and our body starts to relax," answered Garrett. So, Logan and Garrett sat down and tried meditating for ten minutes and then went off to play basketball.

Logan and Garrett met their friends at the basketball court and played for over an hour. "I am glad you came, Logan. You played really well out there," Garrett said. "I'm happy I came too. I was having so much fun I wasn't even worried about breaking my leg," answered Logan.

The two boys laughed. "Looks like meditation helped you today," said Garrett. "I am going to exercise and meditate every day, if I can," was Logan's reply. Logan ended up making the basketball team and even though he still worried sometimes, he used meditation and exercise to help with those feelings.

Throughout the year Logan and his good friend, Nolan, skateboarded to and from school. On the last day of school, Nolan asked Logan, "Do you want to skateboard to Garrett's house for his pool party?" "Nah, I just want to be alone," answered Logan. "Oh, come on, everyone will be there and there is going to be pizza..." Before Nolan could finish, Logan screamed, "I SAID NO!" Nolan was shocked and couldn't believe Logan had yelled at him. This was not like Logan. "Hey, Logan, let's just chill and ride home, and then I'll go to the party," said Nolan, "I think you need a friend right now."

The two boys skated off together, just as they had all year long. As they were coming down the last hill Nolan suddenly hit a rock and fell off his board.

Logan's doctor was able to find medication that helped him manage his moods but it took a while to find the right one. Logan still used exercise, meditation, medication and talking to his family and friends about his feelings. He is no longer ashamed about his depression, anxiety, and anger.

Logan, Danielle, Garrett, and Nolan graduated from high school and went on to college. Although they all have health issues and live miles apart, they are still there for each other in time of need. They all know that your health can be a challenge. It can be a bout with cancer, an imperfect heart, a life-long disease like diabetes or mental health. By sharing their stories, Logan and his friends learned that

"we ALL have something"

and it's important not to hide it and to find ways to take care of ourselves.

GROW · LEARN · REACH
DREAM BIG

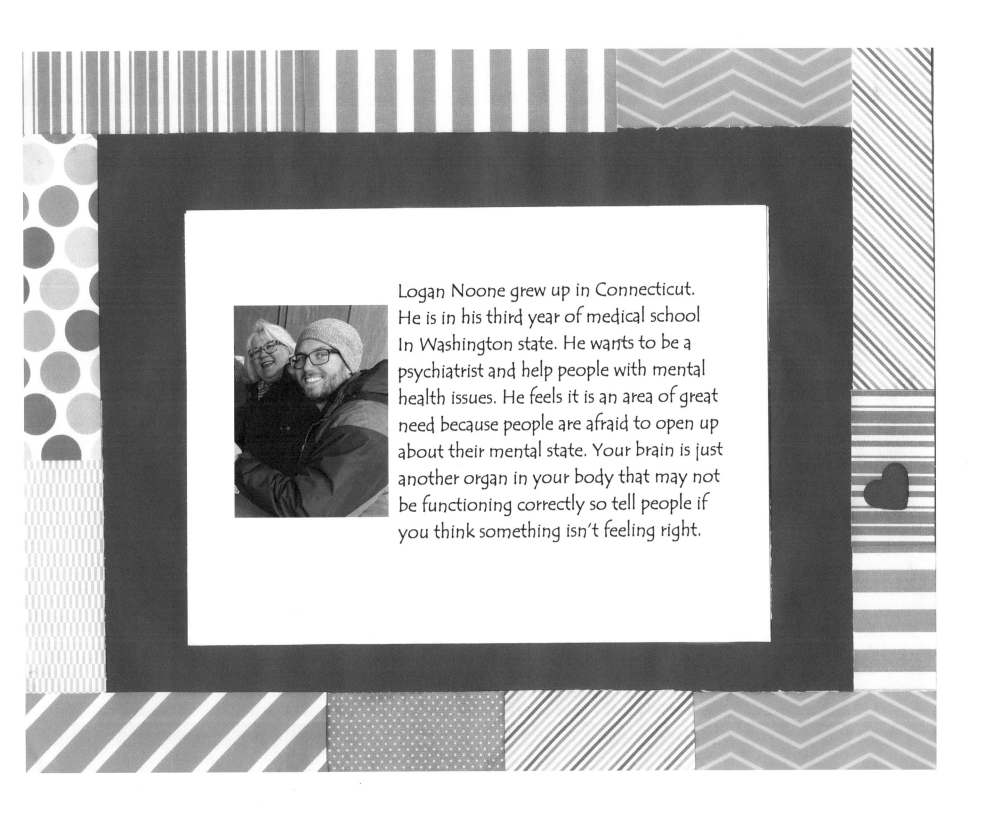

Logan Noone grew up in Connecticut. He is in his third year of medical school In Washington state. He wants to be a psychiatrist and help people with mental health issues. He feels it is an area of great need because people are afraid to open up about their mental state. Your brain is just another organ in your body that may not be functioning correctly so tell people if you think something isn't feeling right.

CPSIA information can be obtained
at www.ICGtesting.com
Printed in the USA
BVHW060540280123
657329BV00001B/1